W9-AUA-912

MoonBall

by **Jane Yolen**

illustrated by

Greg Couch

Simon & Schuster Books for Young Readers

A NOTE FROM THE ARTIST:
I work on museum board; it's like a very thick, smooth water-color paper. I put down many washes of liquid acrylic paint until I get the mood I'm looking for. Then, I add details for the faces, clothes, etc. with colored pencils. If the colors aren't bright enough after that I go back with a small brush and more acrylic and add the finishing touches.

SIMON & SCHUSTER BOOKS FOR YOUNG READERS
An imprint of Simon & Schuster Children's Publishing Division
1230 Avenue of the Americas, New York, New York 10020
Text copyright © 1999 by Jane Yolen
Illustrations copyright © 1999 by Greg Couch
SIMON & SCHUSTER BOOKS FOR YOUNG READERS
is a trademark of Simon & Schuster.
Book design by Paul Zakris
The text for this book is set in 16-point Cooper Medium.
Printed in Hong Kong
First Edition
10 9 8 7 6 5 4 3 2

LIBRARY OF CONGRESS CATALOGING-IN-PUBLICATION DATA
Yolen, Jane.
Moon ball / by Jane Yolen ; illustrated by Greg Couch.
p.   cm.
Summary: Danny always strikes out, but in a dream he
plays baseball with the moon and stars and finds it an eminently satisfying
experience.
ISBN 0-689-81095-4 (hardcover)
[1. Baseball—Fiction. 2. Dreams—Fiction.
3. Outer space—Fiction.] I. Couch, Greg, ill. II. Title.
PZ7.Y78Mo 1999   [E]—dc21   96-44368   CIP   AC

To Adam and Jason and
all those Little League games
—JY

To Emily
—GC

THE afternoon the moon
came out early,
hanging over the field
like a pop fly,
Danny Brower struck out again.
Round-faced and grinning,
the pitcher threw his glove
into the air
to the cheering of his team.
They called Danny names
like Hitless Wonder
and Danny the Whiffer,
while Danny's own teammates groaned.
No one talked to him
when he came back to the bench.
Not even his coach.
In a way, Danny was glad.
If anyone had said something
the least bit nice,
he might have cried.

He trudged home alone,
his glove snugged under his arm.
The memory of jeers and catcalls
echoed in his ears.
He was glad no one in his family
had come to the game this time.

Danny went up to his room
and lay on his bed
for a long, long time;
not sleeping,
just watching the moon
round the bases of the sky.
He remembered every single game
he had ever played.
Just once, he thought,
just once I wish I could hit the ball.
He felt tired,
as if he had played the game
all by himself.
Tired—but not sleepy.

And then, outside, Night's field beckoned.
All at once Danny floated,
glove in hand,
out the open window
to play baseball with the All-Stars.

They greeted him
like an old friend.
"Dan the Man," called Orion.
"My boy!" Dipper cried.
The Gemini twins
gave him a high five.

Rigel laughed
and blew him a kiss,
just like his aunt Alice,
who had played in the minors.
And the rest
of the All-Stars
cheered.

"Let's do it!" came an angry voice.
It was Moon,
his round, white face perspiring.
His team, the Orbits,
echoed him.
"Let's get started," they called,
taking the field.

They threw the ball
around the infield.
Slip-slap, slip-slap, went their gloves.
The base paths glowed.
"Play ball!" cried Moon,
and the game began in earnest.

Ursa hit the first pitch smartly
and got to second,
flashing to the bag
like a meteor to Earth.
Aries singled her to third.
A sharp bunt by Andromeda
filled the bases.
And then it was Danny's turn.

Danny trudged to the plate,
the bat heavy on his shoulder.
"No-hitter," sneered Moon.
"What a whiffer,"
called the shortstop.
Danny knew they were right.
He started to turn,
started to go back
to the bench.
But Rigel was behind him
whispering,
"Eye on the ball is all."
Aunt Alice said that, too.
Said it was
the most important advice
she herself
had ever gotten.

Danny nodded
and smiled weakly at Rigel.
He gave the bat
a few practice swings
then squeezed his eyes
down to slits.
He watched Moon
pick up the resin bag.
Moon passed the bag
back and forth,
back and forth
between his big hands.
Sparks of light
like twinkling stars
shook loose.

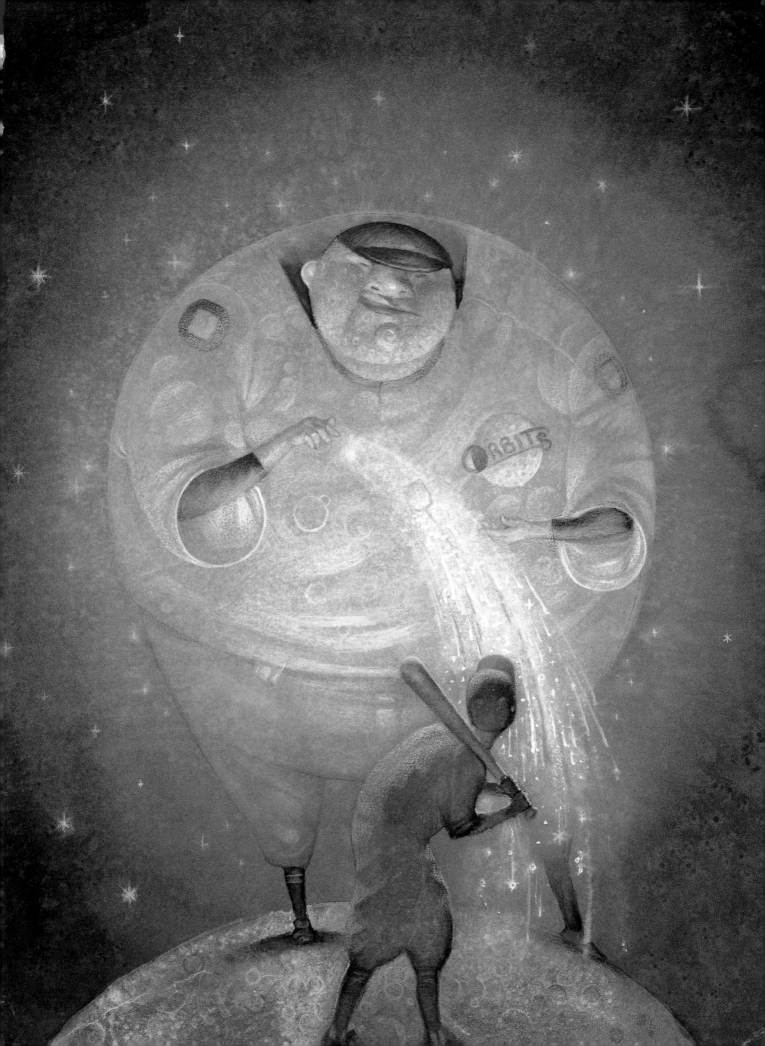

Then Moon dropped the bag,
picked up the ball,
reared back,
and threw.
The ball streaked toward Danny
fast as a comet.
He closed his eyes,
swung hard.
And missed.

"No-hitter!"
Moon laughed.
It was not a nice laugh.
He wound up for his second pitch.
This time the ball came in slow.
Danny blinked,
swung again.
And again he missed.

Moon said nothing.
He did not have to.
Danny already knew
what Moon was thinking.
Moon wound up
and threw the third pitch.
It was a slider.
Suddenly Rigel's voice sang out clear:
"Eye on the ball is all."
And this time
Danny kept his eyes open,
watching the ball all the way.
As it came closer,
it was a sphere,
an orb,
a planet.
It was big and round and beautiful.
He could even see its seams.
Danny swung hard . . .

and connected.
The bat made a sound like thunder
when it hit.
His hands stung
with the power of it.

"Run, Danny, run!" cried Rigel.
Moon threw his glove down
in disgust.

Danny watched the ball
streak across the sky,
falling to the far side of Earth.
A home run!

Danny ran and ran
around the bases:
first,
then second.
He heard the All-Stars cheer,
loud and louder.
All of a sudden they went quiet
like the moment right before sleep.
Eye on the ball,
Danny thought to himself,
that really is all.
He blew a kiss to Rigel as he ran.

Then he rounded third
and floated
on to home plate.
And do you know—
it was as soft
as his own bed,
and somehow
just
as familiar.